BIRDFEEDER BANQUET

BIRDFEEDER BANQUET

Michael Martchenko

Annick Press Ltd., Toronto, Canada

2nd printing, December 1990

Annick Press gratefully acknowledges
the support of The Canada Council and
The Ontario Arts Council

Canadian Cataloguing in Publication Data

Martchenko, Michael.
   Bird feeder banquet.

ISBN 1-55037-147-9 (bound). – ISBN 1-55037-146-0 (pbk.)

I. Title.

PS8576.A77B5 1990   jC813'.54   C90-094542-7
PZ7.M37Bi 1990

Distributed in Canada and the USA by:
Firefly Books Ltd.
250 Sparks Avenue
Willowdale, Ontario, M2H 2S4

♾ This book is printed on acid free paper.

Printed and bound in Canada by
D.W. Friesen & Sons, Ltd.

To Patricia

One day, as Jennie was putting yet another dirty glass into the kitchen sink, she looked out of the window at the bird feeder.

There was lots of action. Birds were fluttering all over it. Seeds were flying in every direction. In fact, there were more seeds on the ground than in the bird feeder.

"Mommy," said Jennie, "I don't think the birds like the seeds. They're throwing them all away!"

"Oh no," said Jennie's mother, "that's the finest blend of grains and sunflower seeds available. What's more, they were selling it at a very good price."

"Hmmm," said Jennie as she put her coat on and went out into the backyard. She reached up into the bird feeder, took out a handful of bird seed and popped it into her mouth. "YUK! PTOOIE! This stuff tastes awful! No wonder the birds won't eat it."

Jennie dashed back into the kitchen. She took out the peanut butter, jams, boxes of ice cream, potato chips with avocado dip, mixed nuts, her favourite breakfast cereal, crunchy cat food and, for good health, she threw in granola, oat bran and chewable vitamins ABCD.

She stuffed it all into two huge shopping bags and dragged them out to the bird feeder.

The next day Jennie looked out the kitchen window. "Wow!" There were birds everywhere, happily squawking and chirping as they gobbled up Jennie's amazing new bird feed mixture.

After a few weeks Jennie noticed there was something strange going on in the backyard. Things started to look like they were made of rubber. The telephone lines drooped down like wet spaghetti. The branches on the trees and bushes all seemed to drag on the ground. The bird feeder was leaning to the left, the fence was leaning to the right, and the cat was acting nervous and wouldn't leave the house.

But the strangest thing was that the birds seemed bigger. They were bigger. They were ENORMOUS!

"Oh oh," said Jennie. "Maybe my amazing new bird feed mixture is *too* good. Those birds just can't stop eating. I'd better not feed them for a while."

Next morning Jennie rushed out of the front door on her way to school. She ran straight into a huge mob of enormous birds. They stared at Jennie. Then they began making a low growly, chirping noise as they pointed at their stomachs.

"Oops, excuse me," said Jennie, "I think I've forgotten something." She dashed back into the house and got a huge bag of her amazing new bird feed mixture.

Meanwhile, all over town, other people began to notice the change in the birds. Enormous birds broke branches when they landed, they used clothes lines as skipping ropes, and they kicked out roof shingles to use as frisbees.

For fun they would chase cats and dogs. They loved to practice dive bombing—their favourite targets were bald men and clean cars. The townspeople had to carry umbrellas, even on sunny days. To top it all off, their loud chirping woke everybody up at the crack of dawn.

The townspeople began to get very upset. They all got together and went to see the Mayor, who was meeting with the Town Council. "Mayor," they said, "you've got to do something about this birdie business!"

The mayor scratched his head.

A town councillor said, "Your Honour, it's Jennie! It's her fault. *She's* got to do something about this birdie business."

The next day Jennie got a huge letter delivered to her house. The letter said, "Jennie, this birdie business is *your* fault and you have to do something about it." It was signed by the Mayor and all of the Town Council.

"This looks serious," thought Jennie. "I'd better do something quickly."

The next day Jennie brought the family tape player into the backyard. She started to play her mother's exercise tape and sure enough, the birds turned up, thinking it was time to eat again.

"Okay, you enormous birds, let's go!" said Jennie. "Three more, two more, one more, shake those tails, stretch those feathers. Make it burn, make it burn."

The birds liked the music at first, then they got bored. So they kicked off their leg warmers and went to find something to eat.

But the next day Jennie had an even better idea. She placed mirrors all over the backyard. She hung them from tree branches, from the bushes and she stuck them in the ground in a circle around the bird feeder.

"Once those greedy eaters see themselves in the mirrors, they'll have had enough," thought Jennie, feeling proud of herself and her brilliant plan.

The birds loved it! They grinned and made faces. They fixed their feathers into all kinds of strange shapes. They showed off, strutted their stuff and moon-walked in front of the mirrors for hours and hours.

"I give up!" yelled Jennie in disgust.

But the birds didn't. They ate anything and everything their eyes could see. They ate hot dogs. They ate jelly doughnuts. They even were seen stopping traffic to eat gum off the streets.

Fall came. The days got cooler. The leaves began to change colour and the birds were bigger than ever.

One afternoon, Jennie went to the garden shed to get a rake. There, in the yard, were all the birds whistling and chirping as they were packing. They were stuffing their backpacks and little travel bags with swimsuits, shorts, sunglasses, straw hats and suntan lotion.

"Yippee," yelled Jennie, "the birds are leaving, they're going south, they're leaving! leaving! leaving!"

She jumped on her bike, peddled as fast as she could to the Town Hall and told the Mayor and all the Town Council.

"The birdie business is over! The problem is solved. THE BIRDS ARE LEAVING TOWN!"

The next morning, bright and early, the Mayor, The Town Council, all the townspeople and the town band went down to the fairgrounds to see the birds off. The band played, the people all cheered, clapped and waved as the birds began to take off.

Abruptly, their cheers became moans and the music turned to groans. Some of the birds flew three or four feet before they fell down exhausted. Others couldn't take off no matter how hard they flapped their wings.

The birds had become TOO ENORMOUS TO FLY! So, they unpacked their bags and decided to stay.

The Mayor turned bright red and began pulling his hair out. The Town Council began to cry. The town band started to pack their instruments. The townspeople stared at Jennie. Jennie was looking for a hole to crawl into when suddenly she jumped up into the air with a huge grin on her face. She ran to the Mayor and whispered into his ear.

The Mayor stopped pulling his hair out. His face lit up. He took Jennie by the hand and went off to find a telephone.

A short time later there was a loud rumbling noise in the sky and suddenly a huge airplane flew in low over the horizon. The plane circled overhead once, then landed on the field in the middle of the fairground.

As it came to a stop, the pilot poked his head out the cockpit window and yelled, "SOUTH BOUND BIRDIE BUFFET— All you can eat. Climb on board!"

All the birds began chattering and chirping and hopping up and down with excitement. They waddled up the ramp and into the plane.

In a few minutes they were all on board, the ramp went up, and the plane took off.

As the plane circled overhead, the Mayor, Town Council, townspeople and the band all waved and cheered—then burst into laughter.

Painted on the other side of the plane were the words, "HEALTH SPA."

"Good thing birds can't read," thought Jennie as she waved.